Shootout at Sanctuary City

A Jack Cordell Western

R. Annan

Jump into the adventures of Jack Cordell by R. Annan.

The Gunfighter in Winter

Long Ride to Hell's Kitchen

Owl Hawks

Gunfight at Barfield Springs

Shootout at Sanctuary City

Last Days of a Gunfighter (*forthcoming*)

Coming soon: Clay Jared Westerns

This one is especially for

Laura

A Daughter and a Friend

1.

Jack Cordell was almost asleep in his seat in the passenger car when the westbound train from Kansas City to Hays City stopped at Topeka. A bunch of passengers got on and as the train started off again someone rudely plunked themselves down on the seat next to him. Cordell looked over and gave the man a stern look.

Only it wasn't a man.

It was a young girl dressed like a man. She wore a wide-brimmed cowboy hat, shirt, suspenders, pants, and boots. She also wore a gun. Her clothes were somewhat shabby and dusty.

She noticed Cordell's irritated look and smiled.

"Sorry, mister," she said in a voice that was musical yet edged with hoarseness. "I didn't mean ta wake ya up."

She pulled her hat down too low for Cordell to see her face. He could see only her mouth and chin. She had a slight overbite that gave her a cute, boyish look. Her auburn colored hair was tucked neatly up into her hat.

She reminded Cordell of a certain girl he met for a brief moment years ago. It was a tragic encounter. She ended up dying in his arms after he busted her out of jail.

"You goin' far?" the cute little pixie asked.

Cordell really didn't feel like talking. He shrugged and sighed.

"Ellsworth," he said.

"I been there once," the girl said. Cordell took her to be twenty, perhaps twenty-five at the most. "It's a shitty town."

"Some people like it," Cordell said.

He looked around the passenger car. It was full now, after that last stop. Two cowboys across the aisle facing them were staring at the girl. When they saw Cordell look back, they pulled their hats down and slumped back in their seats.

"Yer a pasteboard pirate, aincha mister," the girl said.

"A what? Oh, a gambler." Cordell chuckled. "What makes you say that?"

"Yer wearin' a suit," she said, "an' yer hands are all white an' soft lookin'. You ain't no cowboy, thet's fer sure."

Cordell was fully awake now. He sat up.

"Where are you headed, ma'am?" Cordell asked.

The girl burst out laughing. "You sure are a slick talker, mister. Nobody ever called me ma'am before."

"Sorry. I mean to say, miss," Cordell corrected. This only made the girl laugh more.

"Shit! I guess you ain't never seen a cowgirl before, have ya? I ain't no miss, either."

Cordell suddenly admired this girl. She seemed to have no inhibitions. She was like a wild stallion waiting to be broken. But it would be sad if she was. She was a breath of fresh air.

"Where are you from?" Cordell asked.

"Anyplace ya want me ta be, handsome," she said. "You name it, I've been there."

Cordell chuckled. He liked this girl more and more. She was an absolutely blank slate. Straight off the plains. He wondered why she was even on a train. She should be riding a horse with the wind in her hair and rounding up cattle. He stared at her. She stared brazenly back, smiling.

"Are you hungry?"

'Sure. I'm always hungry."

"Would you care to accompany me to the dining car?"

"What?"

"Join me, go with me."

"What fer?"

"Coffee and dessert."

"What the heck's a dessert, mister?"

"Cake or pie."

She suddenly smiled happily. "You buyin'?"

"Of course," Cordell said.

"Okay, then," the girl replied.

Cordell stood up and held out his hand.

"After you, ma'am."

The girl chuckled at the word ma'am again and got up. Cordell noticed the two cowboys were staring. The girl looked at them and winked. They winked back.

Cordell led the girl forward, up one car towards the engine where the dining car was located.

"What's yer handle, mister?" the girl asked.

"Cordell. Jack Cordell."

"They call me Buck-tooth Sarah because of my two big front teeth." She pointed to her mouth. "I'm kinda ashamed of it."

"Why?" Cordell asked. "You're very pretty, Sarah."

They went into the dining car.

A few married couples and a dozen or so businessmen were there. When they saw Cordell and the girl walk in they turned to stare. Some of the women started to snicker with their hands covering their faces. The men chuckled amongst themselves.

Cordell pulled a chair out for the girl. She hesitated then sat down. She was clearly uncomfortable.

"I ain't supposed ta be here, mister. Yer gonna git in trouble because a me."

"You're my guest, Sarah. It's fine." Cordell sat down across from her.

A waiter came up and gave them both a menu. The girl stared at it, shaking her head. She looked about to panic and run.

"What's wrong?"

"I can't read, mister."

"I'll order for the both of us," Cordell said. He ordered a coffee and apple pie for the girl and a coffee for himself.

Everyone was staring, especially the woman. They wore dresses while she wore men's clothes. They wore bonnets and she wore a cowboy hat. What kind of riff-raff was she? And what was this man doing bringing her into the dining room?

When the coffee and pie came, they watched the girl eat. She didn't know how to hold a fork properly and almost dropped it. That resulted in loud snickering.

"Just pick it up and eat it," Cordell said. "And don't pay any attention to these people. They're all snobs."

"I kin see thet, alright," the girl replied.

She picked the pie up in her hands and ate away. Cordell nursed his cup of coffee as he watched her eat like a hungry kid.

After she devoured the pie, the girl gulped down her coffee, and then rolled a cigarette and smoked. This set the other diners chattering and snickering even more.

"Would you like anything else, Sarah?" Cordell asked.

"Hell, I guess a shot of rotgut would sure do good," the girl said.

Cordell ordered two brandies. When they came in small, delicate glasses, Sarah chuckled. She held her glass up and sniffed loudly.

"What the hell is this?"

"Brandy," Cordell said.

"It sure smells somethin' sweet," the girl said and tossed it down in one gulp. She shivered. "Damn if it don't taste like toothache medicine."

Cordell chuckled. "It best to sip it."

Sarah looked around the dining car. Everyone avoided her staring eyes. "Sure is cozy in here. Except fer all the buzzards a gawkin' at me."

"Don't let them get to you, Sarah," Cordell said.

The girl chuckled. "Get ta me? Hell, I reckon I'll be getting' ta them right soon enough."

Cordell didn't know exactly what that meant but he chuckled anyway.

The girl stood up.

"What? Are you leaving me with the buzzards?"

"Yeah. You stay here an' enjoy yer toothache medicine."

She stood there looking at Cordell then spread her arms out, waiting for him to give her a hug. He stood up and they came together. She felt good in his arms. She kissed him lightly on the mouth.

"Thanks fer the education, mister," she said and left.

Cordell sat down and ordered another brandy. The taste of her lips lingered on his. She smelled like fresh grass, unspoiled by civilization, untouched by humans. He wondered where she was going, what her life was like. From all indications, it was not an easy life. Her hands were strong, and she was solid. She was also a real character, but a cute one.

As he sat there thinking about her, the dining car gave a little jerk and seemed to speed up. He didn't think anything about it until later when he reached for his billfold to pay the bill. It was gone.

Luckily, for him he had a pocketful of double eagles.

2.

The bigwigs in Washington really didn't know Senator Andrew Crowley. They knew he was a rising star in the Kansas political constellation, but they didn't know the content of his character.

Born to a Kansas cattle baron father and caring mother, Crowley grew up on a huge ranch.

As a child he developed a cruel streak and liked to torture small animals. The feral cats and stray dogs that hung around the ranch house were often found strangled, gutted, or tortured. His brother, two years older than him, died mysteriously from a fall off a cliff while the two siblings were out hunting together.

In town, Andrew Crowley liked to pick fights. He was very fast with a gun and loved to provoke cowboys into a fight and outdraw them. Especially if they were drunk. He practiced his fast draw for hours every free moment he had.

In order to get the boy out of the way, his father sent him to college. Andrew didn't like this very much so he managed to get tossed out for being a troublemaker on campus. After three western colleges threw him out, his father sent him east to an Ivy League college under the threat of being disowned if he got into trouble there. The boy finally settled down and managed to hang on for four years.

But young Crowley still had a bad temperament and exploded emotionally, even in public. He was easily provoked to anger and responded violently, regardless of where he was or who he was with. This was seen many times on the college debating team where Andrew Crowley became known as, 'Firecracker Andy.' Some debates ended in a duel with pistols in a field behind the men's dorm. Crowley always won.

After college he returned home to Kansas where his father steered him into politics. Crowley could be a charmer if he saw an advantage in it. No one ever saw the real person inside him. He kept that hidden. His father had a lot of connections in the political realm and used those to advance his son's career. He knew where the money was and made the deals to get Andrew elected.

During his first term in office a double tragedy struck. Crowley's parents drowned at sea on a private yacht in a storm. A year later the cattle market collapsed and the price of beef plummeted. It marked the end of the cattle barons. At the advice of his lawyers, Crowley sold off much of his cattle and land, getting it all down to a more manageable size.

It was about that time that Andrew Crowley decided he needed a wife. Preferably one with money and Washington connections. He finally found her in beautiful Laura Metcaf, the daughter of a long respected Maryland family.

Little did she know that Crowley would drive her to drink. And worse.

3.

Elroy Slade was a train robber more by necessity than choice. However his small gang wasn't very successful or very well known. Perhaps Slade's heart wasn't really into it.

One of his men, the Professor, a little old bald-headed man with three fingers missing on his left hand, was a good demolition man who worked for the Union Pacific blasting holes through mountains. It was dangerous work for which he got paid very little so the Professor decided to blast trains for a change. They carried money. Mountains didn't.

The Professor worked on the same railroad crew where Slade was in charge of laying and maintaining tracks. These two close friends saw how the railroad upper crust lived and how they wined and dined politicians and traveled in special railroad cars paneled in expensive wood and fabrics, and had servants. These executives made the foremen push the workers to the brink of exhaustion, and then some.

Slade's wife and young daughter lived in a moveable tent. Once a week they would fold the tent up and load it on a flat car and take it to another location. It was a hard life for both his wife and daughter.

Slade, a big, husky, rough and tumble man, once a ramrod on a small ranch, got respect with his fists and gun. But no matter how much work he got out of his men it just wasn't enough to satisfy his railroad bosses. They demanded more and more.

Slade's wife was a delicate woman and life as the wife of a railroad man eventually took its toll. She died when their daughter Sarah was sixteen, leaving Slade to care for her. Her death left Slade a very bitter man.

One night in tent city, alongside the railroad tracks, Slade and his companion, the Professor, heard two of his men, Ben Parker and Torrey Benton, griping about their wages. They sat down and joined them, listening to what they had to say.

Before long, Tom Drury, Sam Norton, and Dave Thomas came to join them. They passed a bottle around among themselves and talked about the good life the bigwigs at the top were enjoying at their expense. By late that night they all agreed on one thing. They wanted a better life than the one they had. They wanted something much better.

Slade's only problem was that he had a young daughter and no relatives or friends he could leave her with. He would have to take her on any adventure he decided to embark upon, no matter what it was.

One day during a railroad labor dispute the men went on strike. The railroad hung tough and refused to negotiate a small wage increase. They called in Chinese labor and told Slade and his crew they had to work shorter hours.

After a week and no solution, Slade took a vote from his little crew. They decided to get revenge on the railroad. They would rob the hell out of it. Some of his men, such as Ben Parker and Torrey Benton had been cowboys and could ride well.

That left Elroy Slade with one big problem, however, and that was his daughter, young Sarah.

Finally, after wrestling with it for a few days, he told her outright what he planned to do. She said she would never leave him and he swore he would never abandon her. They both cried about their difficult situation.

"Oh, God! What am I gonna do, girl? Help me out on this, baby!"

"I'm a goin' with you, pop," the young girl said, weeping. "Come hell or high water, I'm a stayin' with ya. Mom would want me to." Slade could see the pain in her eyes and hear it in her voice.

"Are you sure?"

"Hell, pop, I kin ride an' shoot with the best of 'em. You know thet! You taught me, didn't ya?"

"I sure did, didn't I, baby," Slade said. "Okay, yer in, kiddo!"

The next day Slade, the Professor, Ben Parker, Torrey Benton, Dave Thomas, Tom Drury, and Sam Norton quit their job on the Union Pacific Railroad. They decided to become train robbers.

Sarah rode off with them.

The Slade gang soon found out that working on a railroad, and robbing one were two different birds. While swinging a sledgehammer took muscle, robbing a train took brains. Of course they did have the advantage of the Professor and they knew trains like the back of their hands. Still, it wasn't easy. It took planning and precision.

With many hundreds of miles of train track and hundreds of trains running along them, it was fairly easy pickings if done right. Kansas, Nebraska, and Wyoming were wide open and the little Slade gang was only one of hundreds of gangs robbing trains for a living.

Their first job was outside Junction City. They hit a Union Pacific train headed for Fort Harker. It had a small civilian payroll stashed in the mail car safe. The Professor's dynamite cut the mail car from the main engine and tender and the Slade gang swooped down, blew the safe, and rode off with eight-hundred dollars. A whole month's wages for all of them. All in double eagles.

Some jobs netted a thousand dollars, some less. But things didn't always go well. Twice they were caught off guard by railroad sharpshooters. On one job they were met by withering gunfire and lost Tom Drury. He caught a bullet in the back and died that same night.

After that Slade made sure Sarah kept out of harm's way. She stayed on the sidelines with the packhorse that carried the dynamite, extra ammunition, and food. His big nightmare was that someday he would find her body laying alongside the railroad tracks, shot to ribbons.

Down the line it got more and more dangerous. They lost Sam Norton when they ran into another ambush. The train had a big payroll and was loaded with armed men.

After that Slade held back for a month.

When he went into action again he concentrated on small passenger trains that ran a route between two points. There were hundreds of those. They carried all sorts of people, including businessmen. Some even had a V.I.P. car. It was usually at the end of the train. The car lineup was, after the engine and tender, a livestock car for the cowboy's horses, the mail car, the dining car, the passenger car, then a V.I.P. car and often a caboose, but not always.

The robbers got less cash on a commuter train, but there were more of them and usually safer to rob.

Slade wasn't going to let Sarah get on a train, but after losing Sam Norton, he was short a man so he gave in to her urging. She would go with his two best men, Ben Parker and Torrey Benton. He gave them instructions to keep an eye on her.

Slade's plan was to rob the commuter train that ran from Kansas City to Hays City. He would drop Sarah, Parker, and Benton off at Topeka at night. He, the Professor, and Dave

Thomas would ride west about twenty miles to a stand of pines and rocks near a bend in the tracks and wait with the horses. They all knew the spot. The train would stop at Topeka and the three would get on. It usually ran late, so Slade, the Professor, and Dave Thomas would have plenty of time to get to the contact point with the horses.

The commuter train would not be guarded, although there might be some brave soul with a gun on it.

That always had to be expected.

4.

Laura Metcaf was the only child of the owner of the Metcaf Furniture Company in Brentwood, Maryland, near the nation's capital. She was an unruly, impulsive girl and a rebellious daughter. Against her wishes, Laura spent her young years in finishing schools throughout the east.

It was while at those various learning institutions that she learned to ride. He parents owned a farm near their factory and had several well-mannered horses just for Laura's use. She often read romance novels about the west and dreamed of someday living on a ranch where life was wild and free.

Her parents often took her with them to the capital where they hobnobbed and rubbed elbows with politicians and bureaucrats. A good government contract could always make the difference between a company surviving or going under. The motto of the Metcaf Furniture Company was, "Furniture fit for a President!" Although mundane, it was very effective. Mr. Metcaf came up with the motto after many days and nights of hard thinking.

Her father, who was aware of the high crime rate in the capital area, bought Laura a cute little .22 caliber pistol. It was nickel-plated, had a pearl handle grip, and fit well into the girl's purse. Laura never left home without it.

The Metcafs had a grand plan for their daughter. They would marry her off to someone with political skills and aspirations, someone on the rise in politics. Someone who might someday reach a high position in Washington. Even someone who might be president.

After Laura was politely asked to leave her last girls academy in Connecticut, the Metcafs decided she would accompany them whenever they got an invitation to, or simply crash, parties in the Washington area.

They were actually husband hunting for their nineteen-year old daughter.

It wasn't an easy task. Laura was very particular. To her all politicians were enemies of the common people, an idea she had gotten from her liberal friends at the Gilmore Academy for Girls. *Down with the bourgeoisie! Up with the downtrodden proletariat! There was no justice for the working class in Washington! Politicians were enemies of the working classes!* So thought young, naïve Laura Metcaf.

However, when she met Senator Andrew Crowley of Kansas, she quickly forgot about politics and social injustices and thought about the far west, open ranges, mountains, herds of buffalo, and all things western. Most of all, she wanted to meet a real honest to God cowboy, a brave man of the west who slept out under the stars. A man who lived by the gun and the code. Actually, she only had a vague idea what the code really was.

Crowley was twelve years older than Laura but that didn't seem to matter to her or her parents. He was of average height, was a bit on the thin side, and sported a pencil mustache and sleeked back black hair.

When a friend of the Metcaf's introduced them to Andrew Crowley one evening at a Washington social gathering, Crowley became struck with Laura's beauty and manners. His late parents had constantly been onto him to marry but he had held off, playing the field. But now he felt ready, and Laura seemed like the 'one.' She more than fit the requirements. She could ride and shoot and she had the regal look a Senator's wife should have.

So, Senator Crowley from Hays City, Kansas, courted Miss Laura Metcaf of Brentwood, Maryland.

At first she was cool to his advances. After all he was a politician, the symbol of all she hated. But those naïve college bred ideas soon gave way to reality as this man of the west courted her in earnest. Also there was the constant pressure from her parents. Although they never came out and said it, they wanted someone else to be responsible for her so they could have some peace and quiet.

After six months of dating, Laura married Senator Andrew Crowley. She really didn't want to, but it pleased her parents. It was a payback for all those difficult years she had given them. Now the slate was clean. Her debt was paid.

She soon learned that being Senator Crowley's wife was not what she thought it would be. They spent very little time at the ranch near Hays City, and were constantly going back and forth to the capital on trains in stuffy V.I.P. cars. They also stayed at stuffy hotel rooms in the Capital.

And Crowley had a very peculiar idea of what a wife was.

From the very start he used her for his own personal advantage. He had her charm certain wealthy gentlemen who he needed to invest in order to promote his career, even if it meant flouting herself conspicuously. She almost felt like a whore.

Sometimes he urged her to work on the wives, too. It all proved distasteful and beneath her dignity. She complained to her parents but they told her it would all smooth itself out and Andrew would settle down after the next election.

He took her campaigning with him and showed her off to the crowds. She spent hours at his campaign headquarters. He had her tell the crowds what a wonderful husband he was.

The pressure finally got too much for Laura and she began to drink more than usual. The embarrassment of being used as an instrument to further her husband's career became too unbearable. She began to feel like a tool he could pick up and lay down whenever he felt like it.

They began to argue and fight over petty things, small insignificant things. They easily got on each other's nerves. Sometimes she feared he would strike her. Often she thought of asking him for a divorce but she didn't want to hurt her parents. She wanted to stay at the ranch and have a normal life with children, lots of children. He didn't. Afraid that she would become with child, the Senator became cold to her. He often visited other women while they were in the Capital, whenever he felt inclined. That's when she would think about the pistol in her purse.

But it all finally came to a resolution one day when Laura Metcaf Crowley fell into the arms of a handsome train robber on the way to Hays City.

From that moment on her life was forever changed.

5.

While Jack Cordell was sitting in the dining car sipping his glass of brandy, and not yet knowing the girl named Sarah had stolen his billfold, Senator Crowley and his wife Laura were sitting in the V.I.P. car, two cars away, at the end of the train.

With them were several wealthy Kansas businessmen, their wives, two railroad executives, a cattleman and a businessman. The Senator was the center of attention and he was listening to their causes and proposals for various projects. A bill for this one and a bill for that one would be much appreciated. Or a piece of government land for a railroad right of way. Perhaps a land grant for more land to graze cattle. Of course there would be a quid pro quo understood, but never outright spoken.

Laura had been through this dance many, many times and she was sick of it. It went against her liberal grain. She often thought of her husband as a political prostitute. One day she would tell him to his face, but for the present she sat in the V.I.P. car watching and listening as Andrew talked and talked to make a point. It bored her to no end.

The wives of the businessmen and the cattleman sat in one little pod discussing the weather and the latest New York City fashions while the men smoked cigars, drank bourbon, made deals, and promised things. When Andrew finally got around to putting out feelers for donations for his next campaign, which was yet two years away, Laura laughed.

"Oh, Andrew," she said, "you're such a whore." She slurred her words a bit. It was the whiskey talking. She suddenly realized she shouldn't have said what she did.

The room went quiet. All heads turned to Laura, then to Crowley, to see what he would do. Would he tolerate such outright disrespect? Was he a man who couldn't control his wife? Anyway, she shouldn't be sitting there by herself staring over at them as if they were animals in a zoo. She obviously needed to be taught a lesson.

The men gave Crowley an inquiring look that asked, "Well, sir, are you going to stand for that? Take charge. Show her who the master is."

When Laura saw the angry glare her husband gave her, she knew her marriage was over. He was about to strike her and if he did, she promised herself, he would never get the chance to do it again. She watched him get up and stick his chest out and straighten his coat in a superior way.

Finally when he had everyone's attention, he walked confidently over to her and leered down at her. She smiled up at him.

"Yes, dear?" she said sweetly.

Crowley's right hand came at her so fast she didn't even see it. She felt a stinging pain in her left cheek. The blow forced her head sideways and it hit the side of the car with a hard cracking sound. She grunted and her whiskey glass flew tumbling to the floor. For a moment she felt very dizzy. The car seemed to spin around and around.

Everyone in the V.I.P. car saw what happened. They watched and waited quietly.

Senator Crowley shoved a finger in his wife's face.

"Watch your mouth, woman!" he growled. His face was screwed up into a demon's mask of anger. She hardly recognized him.

Crowley turned away and smiled smugly. He taught her a lesson, she would not soon forget.

"As I was saying before I was so rudely interrupted, gentlemen," the Senator said as if nothing had happened. He sat down and picked up where he had left off.

Laura Crowley sat holding her cheek. She did not sob, or whine or cry. She didn't apologize or look sheepishly contrite. She just sat there staring blankly at her husband as if he was someone she didn't know. She thought about the pistol in her purse for a moment. No, shooting him would only make her look like a bad person.

The other women looked at her. They huddled together and whispered amongst themselves.

"She had it coming."

"She certainly did."

"I never liked her."

Laura rose up on unsteady legs. She smoothed her pretty pink dress, raised her chin high and marched in a weaving pattern to the door of the car. She hiccupped and stepped out onto the car platform, and was hit with a blast of fresh air. She grabbed onto the railing for support, trying to clear her head. Finally she stepped onto the platform of the commuter car and staggered in, off balance.

She stood there holding the handgrip by the door to keep from falling, realizing how drunk she was. The passengers stared at her. They were mostly tradesmen, businessmen, workers, and cowboys. There were a few women with children, too.

Laura noticed that everyone turned to look at her. They seldom, if ever, got a visitor from the V.I.P. car. Especially a woman in an exquisite, pink, silk dress that would cost them a month's wages.

Laura started off intending to get to the dining car, one more car away, for a cup of black coffee. Perhaps that would ease the pain in her head and clear it. She was in the middle of the car when it lurched a bit and she fell sideways into the lap of a cowboy. His name was Ben Parker.

Parker smiled. Here was a beautiful rich lady sitting in his lap, looking up into his face. He put an arm behind her back to keep her upright. There was the smell of whiskey on her perfect red lips.

The passengers who saw the incident looked on, wondering what the cowboy would do. He was smiling.

"Howdy, ma'am," Parker said. "Where did you come from, heaven?" The passengers all laughed.

Laura looked up at the young cowboy and saw that he was not bad looking at all. In fact, he was quite handsome. She was about to say something when a wave of nausea, caused by the close air in the car, swept over her.

"I need fresh air," she gasped.

The cowboy stood up from a sitting position with Laura in his arms and carried her towards the door, in the direction of the dining room car. Sarah and Torrey Benton gave Parker a puzzled look but said nothing as he passed them.

Benton got up and walked to the opposite end of the car and out onto the rear platform. He was going to separate the commuter car from the V.I.P. car, to kick off the train robbery.

A man opened the door as Parker carried Laura up to it, letting them out onto the car platform. Parker slowly and gently set her down on her feet next to the guardrail. She still kept her arms around his neck.

"Are you alright, ma'am?"

"Yes, I'm fine, thank you, sir."

"You're light as a feather." Parker chuckled.

"Are you a cowboy?"

"Ah, well, you might say thet ma'am," Parker said.

Laura Crowley smiled. He was very nice. She reached up, pulled his head down to hers and kissed him. For a moment Parker thought he was dreaming. He had never been kissed like that before. She pressed her body against his and trembled.

Suddenly Parker felt the car give a little jerk. It began to move faster. He knew that Torrey Benton had detached the commuter car from the V.I.P. car.

"Excuse me ma'am," Parker said, breaking away from Laura.

He stepped carefully down onto the coupling and worked the link pin lose from the dining car end and let it dangle free on its chain. He did the same for the commuter car end. The commuter car slowed down while the dining car went speeding west towards Hays City, still attached to the main train.

Parker got back on the platform next to Laura and grabbed the brake wheel turning it clockwise until the car came to a stop.

"What are you doing?" Laura asked, fascinated.

"I'm robbin' the train, ma'am," Parker said.

"Oh, how delicious!" Laura said.

She grabbed Parker and kissed him again.

Suddenly Slade, the Professor, and Dave Thomas came pounding up with the horses.

Thomas climbed up on the platform, gave Parker a quick inquiring glance, chuckled, pulled his gun, and ran into the commuter car. The Professor looked up from where he sat with the horses and started to laugh. Slade didn't see the humor. He shifted anxiously in his saddle, leering up at Parker and the woman. This wasn't in the game plan.

"Who's this, Parker?" Slade said.

"I ain't got no idea, chief," Parker said. Laura kissed him again. He didn't resist.

Slade climbed up on the platform and went into the commuter car grunting angrily.

A few moments passed. "Maybe you should take her back inside, Ben," the Professor said. "She could get hurt if somebody starts shooting."

Ben Parker nodded.

"You have ta go inside, ma'am," he said. "Come on, I'll take ya."

Parker grabbed Laura's arm and tried to move her toward the car door but she stubbornly refused to budge.

"No! Please!" her voice was urgent and it cut into him. There were tears in her eyes.

Slade, Torrey Benton, Dave Thomas, and Sarah came out of the car and climbed down on the platform steps. Benton carried a sack full of loot.

Sarah stopped for a moment to stare. "By golly Ben, you rascal, you sure got a wild mustang there, aincha?" She jumped on her horse with the others.

"You comin' or a stayin'?" Slade yelled at Parker.

Suddenly a man with a derringer stood in the car doorway and pointed it at Parker. Just as he fired, Laura jumped in front of him, covering his body. Dave Thomas drew from his saddle and shot at the man, winging him in the arm. The man jumped back inside and stayed there.

"Let's go, Ben!" Torrey Benton yelled.

"Are you going to leave me, cowboy?" Laura said softly. She looked pale.

"I'm sorry ma'am," Parker said.

"Come on," Dave Thomas shouted. "We ain't got all day!"

Sarah brought Parker's mount up to the platform steps and he climbed down into the saddle. Laura leaned over and looked pleadingly at him. She reached out.

"Please don't leave me," she pleaded.

Parker grabbed her arm and guided her down behind his saddle. She wrapped her arms around his waist and held fast. The others already started off, all except Sarah.

"Go on, Sarah," Ben said. "Don't wait on me."

Parker nudged his mount into a gentle run. He heard Laura grunt in pain. Sarah rode up alongside him. She looked alarmed. Something was wrong. She stared at Laura, then at Ben.

"What's the matter?" Ben asked.

He dreaded to hear the answer.

6.

"She's been shot, Ben!" Sarah yelled.

"What?"

"She's been hit, Ben! In the side!"

Ben pulled his horse to a stop. Sarah followed suit. She dismounted and helped Laura down. Laura leaned on Parker's horse for support. Her face was very pale.

Slade and the rest stopped up ahead and stared back. Things were going all wrong. This was a train robbery not a train robbery and kidnapping. Kidnapping was a hanging offense in these parts.

The Professor rode back pulling a packhorse.

"You all go on," Sarah said. "We'll catch up later."

"Sure," the Professor said, chuckling.

The Professor got down and went over to Laura. He saw where she had been hit in the side. He got a medicine box from the packhorse and took out a roll of bandage. He looked at the wound.

"Looks like she's been grazed by a twenty-two," the Professor said. "She bleedin' a bit." He wrapped the bandage tightly around her waist. Laura gasped and caught her breath. "This is the best I kin do right now, ma'am."

"I'm fine. Thank you, sir," Laura said.

The Professor nodded and rode up front to join Slade, Benton, and Thomas. They rode off.

"Come on, little darlin'," Parker said. He reached down and grabbed Laura and lifted her up in front of him, into the saddle. She lay back in his arms.

Parker looked over at Sarah as she mounted up.

"Will ya cover me, Sarah?"

"Sure, Ben, I'll cover ya. I promise."

They rode off. Sarah stayed near Ben Parker as the others rode ahead. Half an hour later Dave Thomas came back to them.

"She's holding us up. Either dump her or shoot her!" he growled.

Ben stopped his mount and stared at Thomas.

"Who said?" Parker asked.

"I said! We can't outrun a posses with you nursin' her!"

"Well, I ain't leavin' her," Parker said. He put his arms around Laura.

"Then, I'm gonna plug her," Dave said.

"Go ahead, Dave!" Sarah hissed. "Jest you go ahead and draw! I been wantin' ta plug yer rotten ass for a long time."

Thomas put his hands up and backed off.

"Okay, okay, Sarah honey! Yer the boss."

"Dam right I am," Sarah said.

"In a pig's ass you are!"

Dave Thomas drew. His gun was almost out when Sarah's shot hit him in the chest, knocking him out of the saddle He flipped once and hit the ground with a thud. She rode over and looked down.

"He tried ta take me once, the bastard!" she said, and spit at the body. "Come on, Ben, let's go." She got the bridle of Thomas's horse and they rode over to join the others.

"What happened back there, Sarah?" Slade asked.

"I kilt Dave Thomas."

"Why the hell did you do thet, Sarah?"

"I jest remembered he tried ta take me once."

"Shit," Slade said. "I'd a kilt the son of a bitch myself, had I known thet!"

They rode off at a slower pace.

7.

Jack Cordell felt the dining car give a little hiccup then lurch forward. Someone near the door to the passenger car shouted.

"Hey look! The passenger car broke lose!"

Cordell and the others rushed to look out. Sure enough, the passenger car was getting smaller and smaller as it sat there on the tracks not moving.

"Somebody better tell the engineer!" a man yelled.

The only trouble with that was someone would have to go through the mail car, through the livestock car, and climb over the coal tender. That was no easy task, and dangerous at best.

Another man said, "They'll feel it up front. They'll know right quick. Just wait."

Five minutes later the train began to slow down. It finally came to a stop, held for a moment, and then began to go backwards. By then the passenger car was a good five miles away and out of sight around a bend.

Cordell thought about the girl Sarah and it all started to become clear. Not only was she a pickpocket, she was a train robber. He recalled her last remark, "I'll be getting' ta them pretty soon." He chuckled and smiled to himself. She was indeed an interesting and talented young lady.

Cordell watched as the train gained backward speed. It seemed a long time before they reached the passenger car. It was chaos. People came running out of the passenger car screaming and yelling about being robbed of their billfolds, purses, watches, rings and money.

A railroad guard from the mail car walked down to the passenger car and tried to calm everyone down.

One woman with a newborn child seemed contented. One of the robbers had given her five double eagles. A man with a derringer was slightly wounded in one arm. He said he shot and wounded one of the robbers.

Cordell saw the V.I.P. car down the line. A man was walking up the tracks towards them. In ten minutes he came up to the car and called to the mail guard. The guard came over to where the man sat catching his breath on the platform steps. Cordell stood nearby, curious.

"You alright, Senator?" the mail guard said.

"Yes, yes," the Senator said anxiously. "Have you seen my wife? I think she was either in the passenger car or the dining car."

A man nearby who heard them talking came over. He had his hat in his hand and seemed a bit intimidated by the Senator.

"Speak up!" the Senator barked.

"Was she wearin' a pink silk dress, Senator?"

"Yes!"

The man cleared his throat. He waited. The Senator gave him a double eagle.

"She got on a horse with those robbers," the man said.

"Jumped on or was forced on?"

"Well, I couldn't tell which it were, Senator. But they took her with them fer sure."

"Kidnapped!" the Senator yelled. He turned to the mail guard. "They kidnapped my wife!"

Cordell turned to the man. "Was there a young girl with them, dressed like a cowboy?"

"There sure was, mister," the man said. "It was the same one you took to the dining room. She was in with them robbers, too."

The mail guard gave Cordell a squinty-eyed look.

"Did you know her mister?"

"No, no," Cordell said quickly. "She said she was hungry so I offered to buy her a meal. She, ah, stole my billfold."

The mail guard chuckled. "She sure snickered you good, didn't she, mister."

"Yes, she did."

Senator Crowley stood up and looked around.

"I'm Senator Crowley and I'm offering a thousand dollars reward for the return of my wife!" he shouted. "She was kidnapped from this train!"

"Hell no!" someone answered. "I ain't crazy!"

"Hell, she probably run off on him," a hidden voice said.

"What about you, sir?" the Senator said to Cordell. "You look like an enterprising person."

Before Cordell could answer the mail guard cut in.

"I'll have the mail clerk telegraph into Junction City. It's only twenty-five miles. They'll have a posse out here before sundown, Senator. A big one, once the reward is known."

"Please hurry and do that," the Senator said. "And make the reward two thousand."

After the mail guard left Cordell stood over to one side and rolled a cigarette. He thought about the Senator's wife and the robbers. It seemed odd to him that they would kidnap anyone, let alone a Senator's wife. It was a dangerous game that could end in hanging for all of them when they were caught. And they most certainly would be caught. They would be hounded down like wild animals.

But if the woman wasn't kidnapped then she must have gone willingly, which begged the question, why would she do that? The question bothered Cordell. He would like to know the answer.

And there was that spunky young pixie. She had gotten her hooks into him. Cordell didn't want to see her dangling from the end of a hangman's noose. And he also wanted his billfold back. It had over five hundred dollars in it, the winnings from a month's card playing.

Cordell walked up to the engine cab to see the engineer.

"I'd like to get my horse out of the livestock car."

"You goin' after them?"

"Yeah, that two thousand seems about right," Cordell said.

"Well, don't spend it all at once," the engineer chuckled.

They walked down to the livestock car to get Cordell's horse and gear.

Cordell stood by his horse thinking. He wasn't after the reward. He wanted to see that the girl never swung from a rope. They should be easy tracking. Especially since one of them was wounded. Perhaps the gang would drop him along the way, if he slowed them down. Cordell would find him and maybe get all the information he wanted.

8.

At sundown they stopped alongside a stream deep in a pine forest.

Ben Parker made Laura Crowley a bed of pine and ferns, and laid a blanket over it. The Professor took a closer look at her wound. It was no longer bleeding. He got out the medicine box and with Sarah's help, swabbed it down with some alcohol, and then wrapped it with a clean bandage.

"Sorry I had ta cut yer pretty dress, ma'am," Sarah said.

"It's alright," Laura replied.

"Someday I'd like ta git me a dress like thet. Go to a dance."

Laura looked at this wild girl. She liked her.

"What's your name?"

"Sarah. They call me Buck-tooth Sarah on account of my two big front teeth."

"Well, buck teeth or not, you're very pretty, Sarah."

"Well, I ain't beautiful like you are, ma'am."

"You don't have to call me ma'am. I prefer you call me Laura, Sarah."

"Alright, then, Miss Laura."

Sarah went over by the fire to talk to her father.

"Where we goin' pop?" Sarah asked.

The grizzly old man stroked his stubbly chin.

"We'll stop at Sanctuary City long enough to dump the loot and buy some stuff and then head north for Nebrasky," Slade said. "You ain't never seen Sanctuary City, have ya?'

"No. What is it?"

"Well, it use ta be a minin' town. It's all dried up now except fer ol' Corey Spencer. He used ta rob banks a long time ago. Did ten years in prison an' then went into the mercantile business. Most of the people who live there don't ever leave. They're born there, live there, an' die there."

"No kiddin'?"

"Nope. Ifn you marry one of the clan, you stay with the clan. That's how it is there."

"Gosh."

"Yeah, gosh" Slade chuckled.

The Professor got jerky and hard tack from the packhorse and Torrey Benton made a pot of coffee. Ben brought Laura some food on a bent tin plate and coffee in a bent tin cup. She laughed.

"This is fancy dining," she said. "What is it called?"

"Jerky an' hard tack ma'am," Ben replied.

Laura nibbled politely at the slice of salted beef and sipped her coffee. Ben Parker stared at her. He had never seen such perfection before.

"Yer a lady, aincha?" Ben Parker said.

Laura smiled. "I'd like to think so," she said.

"Yer the only lady I ever met."

"And you're the first gentleman I've ever met."

Ben chuckled. "Shucks! I ain't no gentleman, that's fer sure!"

"You're my knight in shining armor."

"I'm jest a cowboy is all, ma'am."

"Will you be my cowboy, Ben?"

"If ya want me ta be."

"I do. Very much."

"Then I will."

"Do you understand what I really mean, Ben?"

"No ma'am."

"Then I'll show you." Laura whispered.

She leaned towards Ben and kissed him. The cowboy reached for her.

They stopped when Sarah came over to see them.

"You two better stop thet before you set the woods on fire!" Sarah chuckled.

"Whatta ya want?" Ben asked. He looked a little bit embarrassed. He was blushing.

"Pa wants ta talk ta you, lover boy."

Ben got up and went over to where the old outlaw sat alone on a windfall, away from the fire. He seemed in deep thought.

"Ya wanted ta see me, boss?" Ben asked as he sat down next to Slade.

The old outlaw nodded. "When we git ta Sanctuary City yer gonna have ta say adios to her, Ben."

"How come, boss?"

"She's poison. She'll have us all dancin' fer the hangman. Ya see thet, don't ya?"

"Yeah, I guess."

"We got a few more day's ridin', so don't git too stuck on her. It ain't in the cards?"

"I suppose."

"Anyhow, yer a maverick an' she's already been branded. It can't work out. Ya see what I'm sayin'?"

"Yeah, sure, boss."

Slade saw how crestfallen the young man was.

"Look, she can't take you where she's a goin'. It ain't yer world, an' ya wouldn't even like it. It would choke the life outta ya. I'd hate fer that ta happen to ya, Ben."

Ben sighed. "I promised I'd protect her, boss."

"Then you'd best keep thet promise. Go back ta her. Enjoy her whilst ya kin."

Ben stood up to go.

"Don't think I don't like her, I do." Slade said.

"Did you see thet bruise on her face, boss?"

"Yeah, I noticed it."

"When she came runnin' outta thet V.I.P. car, she was holding her face like it hurt."

"Her husband must a slapped her real hard."

"He shouldn't a done it."

"Maybe not, but it's too late ta change it now."

"Well, I'm gonna kill him," Ben said.

Slade chuckled. "Hell, if we ever run across him, I'll help ya. Now go back an' guard yer ladylove. I'm goin' ta bed down."

Ben went back to Laura. She was asleep. He quietly laid down beside her.

They awoke at sun up and broke camp. Laura rode on Dave Thomas's horse in the middle of the group. Sarah was up front with her father and Torrey Benton. Ben Parker brought up the rear, several yards behind, always keeping her in view.

Laura was feeling fully sober now and reality was setting in. Questions rattled around in her mind. What was she doing here? She had made a very rash move. She was in the midst of a small pack of train robbers being chased by a posse. They would be hounded day after day. What if they found out she was the wife of a U.S. Senator? Would they hold her for ransom or perhaps abandon her out here in the wilds?

Slade, the leader, and the girl, Sarah, were father and daughter. What kind of man would raise his daughter as an outlaw? She killed a man in cold blood before her very eyes and never blinked!

And then there was the handsome, young, naïve cowboy, Ben Parker, who fawned over her like a lovesick pup. Her heart went out to him. He treated her like a goddess and risked his life to protect her. She kissed him while she was drunk. Now that she was sober, what should she do?

They were about the same age. She might be a year or two older. When she fell into his lap and felt his arms around her, something happened inside. For the first time in her life it felt right. It felt good. She would have kissed him to death, if nothing had prevented it.

Her thoughts were suddenly interrupted as the boss of the band, Slade, rode back alongside her. He tipped his hat.

"You ride pretty good fer a city slicker, ma'am," Slade said.

"Why thank you, Mr. Slade."

"Excuse me fer askin', ma'am, "Slade said, "but I never did git you full name."

"Laura. Laura Metcaf," she said, giving her maiden name.

"Where ya from, Mrs. Metcaf? Back east?"

Laura knew her eastern accent had been noticed.

"Why, yes, Mr. Slade. How astute of you. I'm from Maryland."

Slade stared at her wedding ring. "I see yer married."

"Yes," Laura said. She suddenly felt cornered.

Slade saw her discomfort and smiled. He'd give her a way out. "Did he do thet to you, ma'am?" Slade pointed to the bruise on her cheek.

"Yes, I'm afraid he did."

"Well, ifn we run into his sorry ass, I'll do the same favor fer him. Only twice as hard."

Slade nudged his horse up front to take the lead again.

But it wasn't over. Torrey Benton took a turn. He rode back alongside Laura.

"Say ma'am, I noticed you a comin' outta thet fancy V.I.P. car. You was wobblin' like a drunk duck, if you don't mind my sayin' it?"

Laura wasn't prepared for that one. It took her a moment to think of a plausible answer. "Yes, my husband and I usually ride in there. He has friends on the railroad."

"What's yer husband do?"

"Oh, he owns a furniture store in Maryland. We have a franchise in Hays City."

The word franchise threw Torrey Benton off balance. He had no idea what a franchise was and was too embarrassed to ask, so he just rode back up front.

They rode half the day and stopped to eat and rest the horses, then went on again. It rained once but not very hard and it soon stopped. It was cooler by evening when they stopped to make camp for the night. After eating, they all sat around the fire. Slade passed a bottle around between him, the Professor, and Torrey Benton.

"Do you have any kids?" Sarah asked Laura.

"No," Laura said. "My husband didn't want any." She paused for a moment. "As it turned out, it was fortunate that we didn't."

They all fell quiet for a while. It started to get colder. They let the fire die out. There was a full moon in the northern sky and it painted the trees and bushes with a silver hue. They soon turned in for the night. Ben got an extra blanket from Dave Thomas's horse and took it to where Laura laid. He carefully placed it over her.

"Stay close to me," she whispered. She patted the blanket next to her. He laid down and she put her small delicate hand into his big rough one. She now knew that the moment she had seen this tall, lean, handsome cowboy she would fall in love with him.

She also knew if her husband every found him he would kill Ben Parker in cold blood and never blink an eye.

9.

"They should be easy tracking," the train engineer told Cordell. "The woman will slow them down. They should be easy to follow."

Cordell nodded. "Unless it rains." He stood by the livestock car stroking his horse's head. It was glad to be on firm ground again.

Clouds begun to gather above, low in a lead colored sky. Lightning flashed in the distance, followed by the rumble of rolling thunder.

"The posse should be out here by tomorrow," the mail guard said.

That was the reason Cordell wasn't going to wait. He wanted to stay ahead of the posse, get as big a jump on it as he could. Maybe he could help the girl out.

Senator Crowley walked over to Cordell as he mounted his horse. "God speed, Mr. Cordell," Crowley said. "Good luck on your quest. Bring her back safe to me and I shall forever be in your debt, sir."

The mail guard said, "If you get her, take her to Junction City. That'll be the closest place."

Suddenly the clerk stuck his head out of the mail car door and yelled to the mail guard. The guard ran over to see what he wanted. They spoke a short while. Just as Cordell was about to start off, the mail guard hollered at him. He went running over to Cordell.

"What's up?" Cordell asked.

"The mail clerk just got a message from Sheriff Cody of Junction City. Seems like there was a break out at Storeyville Prison."

"How does that concern me, friend?"

"Storeyville Prison is about ten miles northwest of where we are right now. They're headed in this direction."

"Who are they? How many?" Cordell asked.

"There's three of them. Mungo Barker, Bull Trainer, and Lackey Barnes."

"I've heard of Barker."

"Yeah," the mail guard said. "He was waiting to be hung for murdering a bank teller and four people in the Coffeeville bank robbery last year."

"What about the other two? Trainer and Barnes?"

"They were slated to hang, too. Barnes killed his wife for cheating with his brother, and Trainer murdered his neighbor's whole family over some stupid disagreement. I don't recall exactly what it was."

Cordell frowned and whistled in disbelief.

The mail clerk went on. "So you'd better be careful. You just might run into them out there. You can never tell."

"Any bounty?"

"Yeah. A thousand for each. Three thousand in all."

Cordell nodded. "Thanks for letting me know."

"Good-luck," the mail guard said.

Cordell nudged his horse across the level area, down into a shallow gully, and up towards a stand of pine trees. That was where some of the passengers said they saw the robbers waiting with the horses.

When he got there he stopped and looked down. There was an empty whiskey bottle and several cigarette butts on the ground, along with some horse droppings. There was a natural opening between the trees that led through to a field. Horse tracks led in that direction.

Cordell looked back at the train, fifty yards away. They were watching him. He waved, they waved back and he rode into the pine stand out of sight.

Cordell wondered to himself why he was doing this. He could just as well have rode into Junction City and taken a hotel room. But that slick little pixie made that impossible. She had his billfold. He was dead broke except for a few eagles left after paying the dining bill. Cordell chuckled. She needed a good spanking. More than that, she needed a new direction in life.

There was also the question of the Senator and his wife. Cordell heard two woman discussing how she latched on to that cowboy in the passenger car. *She practically jumped into the poor man's lap and once she got her hooks into him, wouldn't turn him loose.*

So, maybe it wasn't a train robbery abduction at all. But if it wasn't that, what was it?

And the robbers? They hadn't even tried to rob the mail car, where the real money was. It was as if they were being careful, not wanting to make a big splash or maybe they just didn't have the manpower for a big job.

It was all a puzzle to Cordell.

He rode through the pine stand into a large field beyond. Halfway across it started to rain hard. The heavy downpour washed out the tracks forcing him to guess which way they were going.

Cordell stopped and looked around. Finally he got a telescope out of his saddlebag and scanned the edges of the field, working slowly from left to right. In a few seconds he spotted an opening that led into a stand of aspens on the north side. He rode over to it. When he got there he saw tracks again.

He rode in and about a mile on, the aspens thinned out. He saw another field beyond where a stream ran. It was bordered with grass. When he got there he dismounted and let his horse eat and drink. He rolled a cigarette and smoked it. Finally he got back in the saddle and rode across the field to the other side. There was a wagon trail there that went into a pine forest.

It was raining harder than ever now. Cordell could barely see up ahead because very little light got in between the trees. Gusts of wind blew between the tree trunks and he had to hold onto his hat to keep it from flying away.

Suddenly a man leaped out of the shadows, grabbed Cordell's horse's bridle, and yanked it downward. The animal, startled as much as Cordell was, whinnied, stopped, and pulled back against the pressure. Before Cordell could do anything, someone grabbed his arm, yanked him hard out of the saddle and smashed him in the face with a massive fist. His hat flew off.

Everything turned white, then dark, for Cordell.

"Hold 'em fast Bull! Don't let him git away!" Another man close by yelled.

"Don't worry, Lackey, This son of a bitch ain't a goin' nowhere!" Bull Trainer held Cordell's limp body up to keep him from collapsing.

Lackey turned to Mungo Barker who was having trouble holding onto the horse's head. "What should we do with him, Mungo?"

"Get his gun, you idiot!" Mungo Barker screamed. "And take his money, you ass hole!"

"Okay, boss!" Lackey Barnes stepped over to Cordell and snatched the Colt from its holster and stuck it in his own waistband. After that he began going through all of Cordell's pockets. Finally he stopped and backed away, glaring at Cordell.

"The son of a bitch ain't got nothin'!" Barnes yelled.

"He's most likely got it hidden," Mungo said, grunting under the strain of trying to subdue the horse. "Squeeze it outta him, Bull! Make his eyeballs pop out!"

Bull Trainer chuckled. "Oh, yeah! This is gonna be fun!"

The brute suddenly embraced Cordell, holding him in a bear hug, squeezing him in a vise-like grip. Cordell gasped for air. The veins stood out in his temples as the pressure cut off circulation to his brain. His face turned purple and his eyes began to bulge outward.

Cordell slammed his head forward against Bull Trainer's face. There was a snapping sound as the big man's nose broke like a dry twig. He groaned, released Cordell, and stepped back holding his hands to his face. Cordell did a little dip and came up with his boot knife and drove it into Bull Trainer's belly. The giant gasped and looked down at the handle sticking out of his gut. He sat down in the road with a glazed look in his eyes, wondering how it happened so quickly.

Lackey Barnes pulled the Colt out of his waistband and pointed it at Cordell.

"You son of a bitch! Yer gonna die!" he growled.

Cordell yelled loud. "Kick!"

For a moment the convict was startled.

"What did ya say, ass hole?"

"Kick, boy!" Cordell yelled even louder this time.

Suddenly Cordell's horse raised its two hind legs high and kicked out. Its ironclad rear hooves struck Lackey Barnes in the back with such force they broke his spine in several places. As he fell forward he fired the Colt into the air. He lay all twisted and jerking on the ground. Cordell took the gun out of his hand and shot him in the head, then shot Bull Trainer in the heart.

As he reloaded he heard the sound of a loud bawl. He looked up to see Mungo Barker jamming his heels hard against his horse's barrel, trying to get it to move. Cordell shot him out of the saddle.

After reloading his gun again and putting it in his holster, Cordell ran his hands over his ribs, wincing in pain. They were sore and bruised. He took a few steps, gasped, and inhaled deeply. It required an effort to slowly bend down and pull his boot knife out of Bull Trainer's stomach. He wiped it on the dead man's prison shirt and put it back in his boot.

Cordell stood looking at the scene around him and forced a chuckle. Three thousand dollars reward lay there on the ground and he couldn't do anything about it. Absolutely nothing. Suddenly he went to Mungo Barker. He took his boot knife out again and cut a piece from Barker's prison shirt and stuck it in his coat pocket.

After that Cordell limped to his horse and checked it over. It seemed fine. He hugged its big neck and kissed it on the forehead. It whinnied.

"He tried to hurt you, didn't he pal," Cordell said softly. After a few moments he said, "Kneel, boy."

Cordell's horse bent down on its two front legs making it easy for Cordell to climb into the saddle. Cordell made a clicking sound with his tongue and the horse rose up.

"Good boy!" Cordell patted the horse's neck. "Let's get the hell out of here."

10.

In the middle of the afternoon, on the fifth day after the train robbery, Elroy Slade led his little band of train robbers up a rise and stopped.

Down below was Sanctuary City. It wasn't as impressive as its name, just a mercantile surrounded by log and sod houses. Those looking down could see a few shops and some people walking around. Chickens, hogs, dogs, and a few sheep roamed wild in the one street city.

In spite of its name, it wasn't a city any more. Its reason for existing, the mine, had dried up long ago. It was located way back behind the buildings out of sight, and was now overgrown with weeds, trees, and bushes. Those who lived in Sanctuary City were all connected by blood to the original inhabitants.

For the most part, they kept to themselves. Most of them had no use for the outside world. They never went there unless they needed something from it they didn't have. Then they would send a buckboard to Junction City for whatever it was and quickly return.

Certain illegal entrepreneurs came from various places to deal at Spencer's Mercantile. It was where small time thieves like Elroy Slade dumped their loot at a big discount. Spencer bought it then sold it at a markup in places like Topeka or Junction City. Watches, diamond rings, women's jewelry and earrings ended up for sale in display cases in various towns.

The only thing that stood out as significant in Sanctuary City was Corey Spencer's Mercantile. It was an oasis hidden in the midst of a pine forest, in a far valley in the primitive Kansas outback.

But the Professor decided he wasn't going there.

"I'm going home to Wyoming," the Professor said. "I'm finished with robbing trains, El. Maybe I'll get another railroad job and settle down. Take a wife, perhaps."

"You sure, Bob?" Slade asked. "Have ya thought it over good?"

"Yes, El," the Professor said, using the abbreviated form of Slade's first name. "It's been eating at me for a long time now. I have to go back home. You know what I'm saying El? It's in the blood."

Slade nodded. "Yeah, I guess I do, Bob."

They looked at each other for a moment.

"The time of train robbing' is coming to an end, El," the Professor said. "Take my advice and get out of it. It isn't healthy for Sarah. If you love her, you'll drop it real quick."

"Maybe I will, Bob," Slade said. "Maybe I will."

The professor shook hands with Slade. Ben came up and gave the old man a hug.

"I'm sure gonna miss you, Professor," Ben Parker said. He looked sad. "Be careful now, old friend."

Torrey Benton shook hands with the old man. Sarah hugged and kissed him. He rode north a short distance, turned, waved back at them, and then kept going. Sarah noticed the sad look on her father's face. He had just lost his best friend. She choked back her own tears.

They went down to Sanctuary City, and tied their horses to the rail in front of Spencer's Mercantile and went in. Ben Parker and Torrey Benton went left to get a drink in the bar. Slade shook hands with his old pal Corey Spencer and held up his sack of loot. They went in the back room to tally it up and bargain on a price.

"Come with me," Sarah said to Laura Crowley.

She took the Senator's wife to where the clothing racks were. "I'm gonna turn you into a genuine cowgirl, ma'am," Slade's daughter said, "seein' as you kin ride like one. Where did ya learn ta do thet?"

Laura smiled. "I attended a girl's academy, back east." Suddenly she realized she shouldn't have said that. Sarah acted as if she hadn't heard but she had, and wondered about it.

She picked out a hat, vest, shirt, pants and boots that looked small enough to fit Laura. They took it to the counter.

"I have money," Laura said.

She reached into her purse and pulled out a wad of bank notes. Sarah quickly pushed them back in.

"Lordy, Lordy!" Sarah whispered. "Don't show thet much paper around here! You'll be kilt dead!"

Sarah waited until the clerk tallied up the total then took Cordell's wallet out of the back pocket of her Levi's and paid the bill. After that, Sarah took Laura back behind the racks to change clothes while she stood guard. They left the blood stained dress in a far corner.

"Let's go eat," Sarah said.

Laura followed her to the right and down three steps into a small, attached shack where the smell of stew, fried chicken, and biscuits were strong. There were three cowboys sitting at one of several tables there. They looked up from their food and watched the two women walk over to the serve yourself, all you can eat for an eagle, table.

Sarah and Laura ladled out two bowls full of steaming hot stew and grabbed some biscuits. Sarah tossed a double eagle into the hat and they went to a far table and sat down.

The three cowboys kept staring at them and making remarks amongst themselves. Finally one got up and strutted boldly over and smiled down at Laura.

"Howdy, girl," he drawled with his back arched and his chest puffed out like a rooster. "Mind if I set down?"

"She's married, cowboy," Sarah said flatly in a cold voice.

"Hell, I don't care ifn she is." The cowboy said snidely.

"Jest go back an' sit down there and suck up yer stew, ass hole, before I shoot yer balls off." Sarah said very calmly. The intruder looked confused. This was not at all what he expected.

He glanced over at his pals as if asking for help. They only laughed and looked away. When he saw he wasn't getting any help from his friends, he got all squinty-eyed, and mean. He suddenly turned ugly.

"Who the hell you think yer a talkin' to, bitch?" he asked Sarah.

He swung an open palm and knocked Sarah sideways out of her chair. She went spinning to the floor and sat there looking dazed.

There was a gunshot. Laura reached into her purse and pulled out her pocket pistol and shot the cowboy. She didn't know exactly where. He looked startled, put a hand on his chest, then walked slowly over to his table and sat down. His two companions stared curiously at him.

"She jest shot me with a pea shooter boys! Get me over to the doc's place!"

They quickly assisted the wounded cowboy out of the building.

Sarah got up and stared at Laura with admiration and wonder.

"Well I'll be danged! Thet was quick thinkin' ma'am! You plugged that varmint dead center! You sure did! Let me see that little thing."

Sarah took the pistol from Laura's hand and examined it.

"Where did you git this cute little fellah?"

"My father gave it to me."

"Well, he sure did the right thing, Laura, ma'am. He surely did. Keep this critter close by."

Sarah handed the pistol back. Laura quickly put it back in her purse. Sarah picked up her hat and sat down at the table. They went back to eating again.

"This is very good," Laura said. "What is it called?"

"Skunk stew."

"Oh," Laura said. "Really?"

"Naw, just kiddin'," Sarah chuckled. "It' rabbit."

They finished eating and sat at the table making small talk. Laura asked the girl about her life. She was fascinated by what she heard. Finally Sarah took Cordell's billfold out again and held it up.

"You see this?"

"Yes. What about it?"

"I stole this from the handsomest hombre I ever saw. He's gorgeous. An' I bet he's gonna come an' get it back."

Laura chuckled. "That's very, very clever of you, Sarah. That's one way to get a man to chase you." Laura paused for a moment and laughed. "Ah, are you sure he won't be angry and shoot you?"

"Well, ifn he does, then I'll die a happy woman."

They both laughed. Finally Sarah got up and stretched.

"Let's go see ifn they have anything new in there," she said. "Maybe I'll jest spend all his money on fancy clothes."

They left the beanery and went up the stairs into the mercantile again. Laura followed Sarah in among the racks of clothing. Very little of it was for women, and what they did have was very old fashioned.

Suddenly they heard the sound of horses coming down the rise. It stopped in the front of the mercantile. Sarah froze and stared towards the door.

"What's wrong, Sara?" Laura asked.

"Thet could be the posse!"

Sarah put her hand down by her gun and waited.

11.

Boots pounded up the steps onto the porch and stopped. Someone outside spoke in a loud deep voice.

"You men keep yer eyes peeled while Dave, Buck, an' me take care of business."

"Sure boss," someone outside chuckled. "Ifn there's any gals in there, send 'em out. Even the ugly ones." That remark was followed by laughter.

Sarah looked at Laura. "Pull yer hat down ta hide yer face." She pulled her own hat lower. "Keep low."

"Is it the posse?" Laura asked.

"No, but it could be jest as bad," Sarah said grimly.

The two women stood behind the clothing rack as three men came into the mercantile.

The leader stood out. He was a tall, handsome, dark faced man with deep-set blazing eye. He wore black from his hat to his black leather gloves, to his boots. A single gun hung from his side. The men beside him were plain cowboys, one tall and skinny, the other short and stocky. But the leader was unmistakably a gunslinger. He exuded confidence and authority.

As he looked around the mercantile, checking the layout, he noted the beanery to his right and the barroom to his left.

"Kin I help ya mister?" the clerk at the counter asked.

"Is Spencer in?" the leader asked.

"He's in the back right now. Should I call him?"

"Naw," the man said. "When he comes out jest tell him Earl Gadden is in the bar."

Gadden and his two men sauntered slowly to the left and down the three steps into the barroom as if they were in no hurry. They went over to the counter and lined up at the bar. The bartender, an old bent over, hip-slung cowboy, got up from a chair behind the counter, and ambled slowly up to them on bowed legs.

"A bottle of rotgut," Gadden said. He dropped a double eagle on the bar. The old man got a bottle, three glasses, took the money, and sat down. He quickly began to nod off. In seconds he was snoring. Gadden poured another drink.

"Lookit thet," one of the cowboys chuckled.

"The old fart is out like a light," the other said.

Gadden chuckled and looked around. "This dump ain't changed none since I was last here."

He noticed Ben Parker and Torrey Benton over in a far corner drinking and talking to themselves. They glanced over at Gadden and his two men. He nodded at them in a friendly way. They nodded back and went on drinking and talking.

"We gonna stay here long, boss?" the skinny cowboy on Gadden's left asked.

"That all depends."

"On what?" the short cowboy on his right asked.

"On whether Mungo, Bull, and Lackey make it. They're supposed ta be here today."

"What if the posse got 'em, boss?" the tall one asked. "What then?"

"It'll mess up our plans fer that Ellsworth job is what. I'll need Mungo to blow the safe. As fer Bull and Lackey, I don't give a shit about those two ass holes. They don't have half a brain between the two of 'em."

The short one chuckled. "I heard there's a few good looking women livin' here."

"They're probably all married," the tall one said.

"Hell, I don't care about thet. I'll jest shoot their husbands an' unmarry 'em." He laughed at his own joke.

"We can't stay long," Gadden said. "The posse is bound ta show up. We gotta do the Ellsworth bank job and head fer Mexico real pronto."

The other two nodded.

"Whatta we gonna do about ammo and food, boss," the tall one asked. "We're almost out. Whiskey, too."

"There's plenty of that here," Gadden said. "We'll stock up on enough supplies ta git us to Mexico."

Just then Elroy Slade and Corey Spencer came out of the back room. They stood next to the counter and shook hands. Both seemed pleased at the deal they had struck.

"Let's drink on it," Slade said.

"Sure," Spencer said. "It's on me."

"Someone is waitin' in the bar fer you, Mr. Spencer," the kid at the counter said. "Name's Earl Gadden."

When he heard Gadden's name, Slade stiffened. A tortured, angry look came over his face. He put his hand down by his gun as he followed Spencer slowly into the barroom.

When Slade saw Gadden he stopped several feet away and stared at him.

Spencer, however, walked up to Gadden and offered him his hand. As they shook, Gadden stared over at Slade.

There was a sudden tension in the room.

"Hi, Gadden," Spencer said.

When he saw the old bartender was asleep, Spencer went around behind the bar and got a bottle and two glasses. He poured himself and Slade a shot of whiskey.

Gadden and Slade never took their eyes off each other the whole time.

When Slade didn't come over to get his drink, Spencer knew something was wrong. He could feel it.

He stared first at Spencer, then at Slade.

"What's going on, Slade?" Spencer asked. The old outlaw ignored him. He seemed in a trance as he glared at Gadden.

Gadden stepped away from the bar and faced Slade.

"Hello, Slade," Gadden said calmly.

"Hello Gadden, you son of a bitch!" Slade said through clenched teeth.

The two men drew.

Gadden was faster. He fired a single shot that hit the old train robber low in the chest. Slade never even got his gun out. He sat down with a vacant look on his face.

Sarah and Laura were standing in the saloon entrance when it happened. Wide-eyed and horrified, the young girl ran to her father and knelt at his side holding his big calloused hand in hers. She was in total shock. Tears started to come. The old outlaw looked up at her and smiled weakly.

"Don't cry," the old outlaw muttered faintly.

"Stop talkin'," Sarah said. She looked up and cried, "Somebody help him."

Spencer came quickly around the bar and knelt by Slade's side and opened his shirt. The old bartender came with a towel. Spencer pressed it against the wound to stop the bleeding. Ben Parker and Torrey Benton came over to look at their boss. Gadden's two men watched them closely, their hands down by their guns, ready to draw.

Gadden reloaded his gun and put it away. He stared at Sarah.

"You with him?"

"Yeah, I'm his girl," Sarah said, choking back tears.

She gently released Slade's hand and stood up facing Gadden, glaring hatefully at him.

Gadden looked surprised. "His girl? Yer kinda young ta be his girl, aincha?"

"I mean his daughter, you ass hole!"

"His daughter?" Gadden looked shocked.

"Thet's right," Sarah said. "Draw, you son of a bitch!" she yelled.

"Gadden, don't!" Slade groaned painfully.

Staring at Sarah as if trying to remember if he'd seen her before. Gadden's face softened.

"Come on you bastard! Draw or I'm gonna drill ya right where yer standin'!"

Gadden stood as if all the anger and hate had suddenly drained out of him. His gun hand hung slack at his side.

There was a strange smile on his lips, as if overcome by a sudden, clear vison.

"You've got her looks an' thet's fer sure," Gadden said softly.

Sarah wasn't listening. She shot Earl Gadden in the chest. He grunted, sank to his knees, and forced a smile.

"I really did love yer mom," Gadden whispered.

Sarah seemed not to hear. She fired two more bullets into his chest. He fell sideways and didn't move. She put her gun away.

"You just kilt yer dad!" Slade whispered, in a forced voice.

"What?" Sarah asked in disbelief.

"He was yer dad," Slade muttered. He was pale faced and his breathing was short and shallow.

Sarah looked from one man to the other. She kept looking back and forth, unable to absorb what had just happened, what she'd just done. Then it hit her like an overwhelming avalanche, crushing her and smothering her. She looked up and wailed like a wounded animal. She put her hands to her temples and screamed, pulling her hair and striking herself in the face.

"Oh, God! Oh, God! Oh, God!" she kept crying out. "What have I done? What have I done?"

She dropped exhausted to her knees and sobbed.

"He knew yer momma," Slade said haltingly. "They were lovers once, a long time ago. He's yer real dad. I raised ya when he ran off on her."

The old outlaw coughed. Blood bubbled from the corner of his mouth and he let out a long, slow sigh. His eyes went dull and he died.

Sarah leaned down and put her head on Slade's shoulder. Her body shook from sobbing. Laura came over and knelt next to her, putting an arm around her, holding her. They were both sobbing.

Gadden's men walked over to his body.

"This ain't over," the tall one said. "You'll all get what's a comin' to ya, an' real quick."

They picked Gadden's body up and started for the door. Ben opened and closed it after them. He peeked outside as he did so.

"There were about a dozen of them," he said. "I think we're in for a shootout."

"How many do we have?" Torrey Benton wondered.

"Less than half thet many," Ben said.

They waited for the call to come. In a few moments they heard it loud and clear.

"Send thet bitch out!" someone in the yard yelled. "If we have ta come fer her yer all dead!"

"Hell, I ain't afraid ta brace them ass holes," Sarah said.

She got up and wiped the tears from her face. She reloaded her Colt then made a step towards the door. Ben and Torrey grabbed her arm and pulled her back. Spencer blocked the door.

"You ain't goin' no place, girl," Spencer said. "I've dealt with murderers like this before. They'll kill us all, ifn we let em."

"That's right," Ben said. "We gotta stick together."

The old bartender hobbled up to them.

"What's a goin' on, Corey?"

"We got us a shootout comin' up," Spencer said. "Go git the cook."

"Didn't we jest have one a while back?"

"Yeah, but this is a new one."

The old man scampered away complaining. "Gosh dang it! It's jest one shootout after another. I can't get no sleep around here anymore!"

Spencer chuckled. "He a little batty, but he's good with a rifle." The back door slammed hard. "The kid jest lit out. He can't shoot worth a damn, anyway."

Someone outside yelled, "Let 'em taste lead, boys!"

"Duck!" Ben yelled and pulled Laura down.

A moment later a rain of bullets smashed into the front of the mercantile shattering windows and smashing into the pine board walls. Spencer crawled over behind the counter. He reached up to the rifle rack and started pulling down the rifles that were for sale.

"Everybody get a rifle," Spencer said. "There's plenty of ammo under the counter. Jest dig in."

Another fusillade of bullets raked the front of the mercantile. Bullets tore into the front of the counter and the back wall above their heads. There was a short pause and then they heard men running up the porch steps. The front door flew open.

Ben, Torrey, and Spencer leaned over the counter and levered shot after shot at the open door. The cook and the old man knelt each on one side of the counter and did the same. When the smoke cleared two of Gadden's men lay sprawled dead on the porch.

The old man chuckled. "Thet'll teach them buzzards whose boss around here, by golly!"

Another barrage of bullets came blasting against the front of the building again. Splinters flew into the air like rain.

After that there was an eerie silence.

"The back!" Ben yelled. "They're coming in the back door!"

He and Spence ran back to the storeroom. Just as they got there, they met two of Gadden's men already inside. Ben held his rife low and snapped off a round. It caught one attacker in the side. He levered another round in and shot him again. Spencer took a bullet high on his left arm but was able to drop the second attacker with a shot to the head.

"You hurt bad Spencer?" Ben asked.

"Naw. Let's barricade the door," Spencer said. They dragged the bodies outside and then quickly closed the door, shoving shelves and boxes in front of it until it was blocked.

"I'll send the cook and the old man in here," Spencer said. Ben nodded.

They heard more firing so they bent low as they ran into the front of the store. Gadden's men were pouring round after round into the building. Finally they stopped.

"Let's burn 'em out!" someone outside yelled.

"Sure," someone with more sense said, "then we get no food or ammo. That's real smart!"

12.

Cordell came across a large mass of hoof prints leading off towards the northwest and decided to follow them. About five miles on he heard gunfire up ahead. He nudged his horse into a sprint and a few minutes later he came up on top of a rise. He stopped to look down.

From what Cordell saw, he figured a large building was under siege by a band of about fifteen armed men. They just rushed the front, but were met with heavy resistance and were forced to fall back.

Cordell dismounted slowly. His ribs were still a little sore from the bear hug Bull Trainer had given him. He got out his telescope, and scanned the area, wondering who the good guys were and who the bad guys were. It was hard to tell from this distance. He didn't see any badges or any other signs that indicated the attackers were on the side of the law.

From their ragged appearance they looked more like outlaws trying to take over the building.

It would be dark soon. Cordell stood at the top of the rise thinking about the situation below. He could mount up and go on. If he did that he might be leaving good people inside that building to their death. Finally he came to a decision.

He tied his horse to a tree, sat down, and rolled a cigarette. It was now quiet below and getting darker by the minute. By the time he was finished smoking it was almost pitch black except for the light of a partial moon.

Cordell got up and began walking slowly. He made his way quietly down to the building staying low to the ground, coming up to the far side, away from the fighting. There was a window there and he was able to look in.

Although it was darker inside, he could see shadowy shapes moving. Someone lit a cigarette, and when the match flared up he saw, or thought he saw, Sarah's face in the light. Or maybe it was his imagination. He was tired and sore, so it could be. Or maybe not.

He tried to lift the window. It wouldn't budge. He thought for a moment then crouched down again and walked to the back of the building. There was a door there. He tried to open it and was met with a gun blast. A bullet passed by, missing his head by inches.

"Hey! Anybody! I'm a friend!" Cordell whispered.

"All the friends are in here, ass hole," a voice said. Someone with him chuckled then fired another shot. This one narrowly missed his left shoulder.

"Is there a girl named Sarah in there?" Cordell asked.

"Yeah! So what?"

"Tell her Jack Cordell wants his wallet back!"

There was mumbling inside for a few moments. Then the sound of footsteps leaving. In a few more moments they came back.

"Is thet really you, handsome?"

"Yep, it's me, beautiful," Jack whispered. "Can I come in?"

"You sure kin!"

There was the sound of objects being pushed and shoved and eventually the door opened. Cordell stepped into the shadows. The door quickly closed behind him. Sarah came hard at him and kissed him. He held her close. She was shaking and crying. He put a hand to her face and felt her hot tears.

"My dad is dead," she said.

He held her until she took his hand and led him out towards the front of the mercantile.

"Stay low," she whispered.

Ben Parker met them near the counter.

"Who's thet, Sarah?"

"I got us another gun, Ben," Sarah said.

"We sure kin use one."

"Is Senator Crowley's wife with you?" Cordell asked the young cowboy.

"Is thet who she is?" Parker asked.

"Yeah. A posse is looking for her."

Ben Parker whistled. "That figures."

"What's goin' on here?" Cordell asked. "Who's outside?"

"The Gadden gang," Spencer said.

"Sarah kilt their boss," Torrey Benton said.

Cordell looked at Sarah and chuckled. "You just can't behave like a lady, can you, sweetheart?"

"How about you teach me, handsome?" Sarah said wiping her cheeks dry.

"How come they're not burning the place?" Cordell asked.

"They want the ammo and food," Spencer said.

"That figures," Cordell chuckled.

The firing seemed to have ended for the night.

Sarah pointed to the counter. "The lady is over there. Come on." They crawled over behind the counter.

"This is Jack Cordell, a friend," Sarah said.

"Hello, Mr. Cordell," Laura said wearily. It was evident she was under stress. Cordell could see her silhouette in the darkness.

"Are you alright, ma'am?" Cordell asked.

"Yes. I'm fine."

"I saw your husband some days ago. There's a posse coming to rescue you."

Cordell watched as she shook her head.

"I don't need to be rescued, Mr. Cordell. I'm here because I chose to be here. No one forced me to come."

"You weren't kidnapped?"

"No. Absolutely not."

"Your husband assumed you were taken by force. He's offered a two thousand dollar reward for your return."

"Then he's wasting his money."

Cordell nodded. "I see."

"No, I don't think you do, Mr. Cordell," Laura said. "I hate my husband. I hate him so much I'll kill myself before I go back to him."

"You don't have to, ma'am," Sarah said.

"If my husband sent you, Mr. Cordell, then you should go back and tell him I'm finished with him. I'll be filing for a divorce as soon as I can."

Cordell chuckled. "I can't, ma'am. There's a little rascal here that's got her hooks into me. And as far as your husband goes, I'm not on his side."

Laura sighed. "Then I guess we have something in common, Mr. Cordell. There's a cowboy here who has his hooks, as you say, into me, too." She paused a moment. "I'll never leave him."

Cordell stared at the Senator's wife for a moment and nodded. "I can and do understand what you're saying ma'am, and I wish you good luck with it."

He and Sarah crawled over to see Ben Parker and Torrey Benton.

"So, I guess you're the lucky man, huh?"

"Yeah," Ben chuckled. "Why?"

"You're probably going to hang, lucky man," Cordell chuckled. "Is it worth it? To hang for a lady?"

"Hell, yes," Ben chortled. "She might be a lady, but she sure don't kiss like one!"

Cordell chuckled. "I think I get your point, my friend."

Out front they started firing again. The bullets came lower this time.

"Scatter," Cordell yelled.

Ben grunted as a dozen bullets tore into the mercantile.

"Ben's hurt!" Torrey Benton yelled.

Cordell crawled around in the dark and found Ben holding his right shoulder.

"Crap!" Parker moaned painfully. "It's my shootin' arm, too, damn it!"

Laura crawled from behind the counter with the medicine box. Cordell tore Ben's shirt open so she could get at the wound.

"Don't you die on me, cowboy," Laura sobbed.

"Don't you worry ma'am," Ben said. "I won't."

"Stop calling me ma'am," Laura said, trying to sound casual. "Why, we're practically man and wife."

She kept working on the wound and finally wrapped it up. After that she cradled the young cowboy in her arm, holding him close.

There were three more attacks before dawn. The defenders held fast.

Then, at sun up, there was suddenly a lot of activity out in the yard. Men were shouting and running around. Horses whinnied and pounded the ground with their hooves. Finally someone gave the order to ride and the outlaws rode away in a thunder of pounding hoof beats.

The sound gradually grew fainter and fainter until it was only a whisper on the wind. Everyone in the mercantile stood up and gave a collective sigh.

"They're gone," Torrey Benton cried. "Hot dog!"

Ben and Cordell went to the door and opened it.

"Damn!" Ben said.

There were bodies on the porch and in the yard. The invaders had paid a heavy toll and gotten nothing for it. A third of the Gadden gang were now dead.

The rest came out on the porch. Laura saw the bodies and gasped. She went to Sarah and they hugged.

"Christ," the old man said, "all this and fer what? They didn't git a dang thing."

As they turned to go inside, they heard distant thunder.

"It sounds like it's going to rain," Spencer said.

"No," Ben said. "That's horses. A whole lot of 'em. An' they're a comin' this way."

"It's the posse," Cordell said. "They're coming for Mrs. Crowley."

Laura and Ben looked at each other.

13.

Cordell watched Ben's face. The young cowboy looked lost.

"I kinda figured it was too good ta last," Ben said sadly. "Me bein' a cowboy and an outlaw, and her bein' a lady."

He went into the mercantile. Laura, Sarah, and the rest followed.

It wasn't long before the posse came pounding up into the yard and dismounted. Cordell went to the window and looked out. He nodded.

"Your husband is here, Mrs. Crowley."

Laura looked at Cordell. "As I have already said, sir, I'm not going with my husband. I'm finished with him."

"Then you had best speak to the Sheriff, ma'am. Let him deal with it."

"I'll speak to anyone except my husband," Laura said.

They could hear voices in the yard.

"Jesus," someone said. "I ain't seen thet many bodies since the Billing's Ranch war!"

"Anyone inside?" someone else yelled. "I'm Sheriff Cody from Junction City! Mrs. Crowley? Are you in there?"

"Yes, I'm here, Sheriff," Laura called back.

There were footsteps on the porch. A tall, lean man with a Sheriff's badge came into the mercantile and stood looking around. He had silver gray sideburns and wore a white, wide brimmed hat.

Andrew Crowley brushed past him and stopped.

"Laura, darling!" Crowley yelled and rushed to embrace his wife. He was met with a slap in the face. It stopped him cold in his tracks.

Laura walked over to Ben Parker and kissed him. She turned to look at her husband. "I don't love you, Andrew and I want a divorce."

Crowley was both stunned and embarrassed. He stepped over and squinted at Ben Parker.

"Who the hell are you, fellah?"

Before Ben could answer, Laura said. "He saved me from those robbers out there, the ones dead on the porch."

"All by himself?" the Sheriff asked.

"No, these good people helped too," Laura said.

"Yer dang right we did," the old man said. "Yer dang right!"

"That's right," Spencer said. "So just you run along, Sheriff."

The Sheriff chuckled. "Sure, Corey. Right after the dust settles." He looked at Laura. "Can you tell me what all happened here, Mrs. Crowley?"

"Yes," she said. She spoke haltingly, choosing her words carefully. "The outlaws Slade and Gadden brought me out here to hold me for ransom. These two cowboys, Ben and Torrey shot them both."

The Sheriff chuckled. He removed his hat and scratched his head. He looked around at the others.

"So that's what happened, did it?" They all nodded. "Well, I've been looking for Gadden. He arranged for three convicts to escape from Storeyville Prison. They're still on the loose, so be careful."

"Ah, not any more, Sheriff," Cordell said.

The sheriff turned and stared at Cordell.

"Who are you, mister?"

"Jack Cordell. Those three convicts jumped me a few days back. I managed to kill all three."

The Sheriff chuckled. "Sure you did, mister."

Cordell took the piece of cloth from his pocket. "I cut this from Mungo Barker's prison shirt."

He handed the cloth to the Sheriff.

"Well, I'll be damned. All three, you say?"

"Yep. Mungo, Bull, and Lackey. All three. And that amounts to three thousand in reward, doesn't it?"

"When and if we find the bodies and the wolves an' bears ain't got 'em, sure."

Suddenly Crowley exploded with anger at Ben Parker.

"Stand away from my wife, sir!"

"Go to hell, mister," Ben replied.

"I'm a United States Senator, I'll have you know, cowboy! You had better watch how you talk to me!"

"Kiss my cowboy ass," Ben said calmly.

"What did you just say?"

"I said kiss my cowboy ass, Senator."

Crowley went up to Parker and slapped him across the face. The cowboy stepped back and felt his jaw. He chuckled.

"What the hell kind of a punch was thet?" Ben asked.

"I'm challenging you to a duel, sir," the Senator said.

"You mean yer a bracin' me, mister?"

"Yes," Crowley said. "Unless you're a coward and refuse to fight me."

He rushed out to the yard, took a belt and gun from one of the bodies and buckled it on. He checked the cylinder and reloaded from the bullets in the belt, and then took up a position in the yard.

"I'm waiting cowboy!" Crowley yelled up at the mercantile.

Laura looked terrified. "Don't go out there, Ben. You're wounded. It won't be fair."

Ben checked his Colt.

"Sheriff! Stop this," Laura pleaded.

"I can't, ma'am, unless the cowboy wants me to."

"Hell, no!" Ben said. He looked pale and was unsteady on his feet from loss of blood.

Laura looked around the room. "Please, somebody do something. Stop him!" She grabbed the cowboy's hand. "Please Ben, if you love me, don't go out there."

Sarah came over to Laura. "You got it all wrong, ma'am," she said. "Thet's exactly why he's gotta face him. If he didn't everybody would call him a coward."

"I don't care what they call him as long as he's not dead!"

The Senator called out again. "I'm waiting, cowboy! Or are you afraid?"

Ben pulled away from Laura and went out into the yard. The rest followed, stopping to stand on the porch. The Sheriff went down into the yard.

"Give them some room, men," he told his deputies. "There's gonna be a shootout, so stay clear."

The men grabbed the reins of their horses and made a wide opening in the yard for the Senator and Ben.

The Senator looked across at the cowboy and laughed. "I'll kill him slow, Laura, so you can see him die."

Crowley was ready. He took up the stance, his legs braced and his right hand down just below his holster. He felt good. It was like old times again. He hadn't killed a man in quite a while and wanted to feel that thrill again.

Suddenly Laura came running down the porch steps to Ben. He kept shifting his weight and was having difficulty standing.

"Move away from him, Laura," Crowley yelled.

"Please, Andrew," Laura sobbed. "Don't kill him. I'll do anything you want. I'll go back with you."

"It's too late now, my dear," Crowley said. "You've made a cuckold of me and I cannot let that stand. My honor is at stake here, you know?"

Laura put her arms around Ben. He could hardly stand up. He tried to push her away.

"Please, ma'am," Ben said weakly. "Please."

A voice spoke out. "Okay, Senator, you've made your point." It was Jack Cordell. He came slowly down the porch steps into the yard. "This man can barely stand. There's no glory in killing a wounded man who can't even draw, is there Senator?"

"Have I seen you before, sir?" The Senator didn't remember Cordell from the passenger train. "You look familiar, sir."

"Jack Cordell, Senator. We met at the train."

"Oh, yes," the Senator said dryly. "What's your interest in this matter, Mr. Cordell?"

Cordell removed his coat and dropped it on the porch steps. He turned to Crowley and smiled.

"I guess it's all about fair play, Senator. I've always been interested in fair play."

Crowley chuckled. "I would advise you to reconsider meddling in here. You could get hurt."

Cordell walked over and stood alongside Laura and Ben, but a few feet to one side.

"I'm standing in for the cowboy Senator," Cordell said.

"I have no quarrel with you, Mr. Cordell."

"If I insult you bad enough, will that do it?"

"I'm quite sure it would, sir," Crowley said. "I've killed men for less."

Cordell nodded. "That's what I thought."

Cordell stood smiling, staring across the distance between him and the Senator. The Senator stared back and waited.

"Well, spit it out, Mr. Cordell." Crowley said.

"You're a lowdown, crooked, cheating, ass-kissing politician, and I hate politicians, Senator."

Crowley chuckled. "Very good, Mr. Cordell. Now I'll kill you and the stupid little cowboy you are so vainly defending. Then I'll take my wife home and rape her."

"Senator," Cordell said, "if you draw you'll never ride out of here alive. I promise you."

Crowley looked around, pretending to laugh, in a move meant to distract Cordell. He drew quickly and almost had his gun out, but not quite.

Cordell's bullet smashed into his chest jarring his whole body. For a moment he didn't realize what just happened. He looked down to where he was shot and put his fingers against the wound. When he saw the blood on them he sank to his knees and fired his gun into the ground. His eyes rolled up in his head and he slumped slowly over on his side and died.

Cordell reloaded his Colt and put it back in its holster. He walked over to Laura and Ben.

"Let's get him inside," Cordell said.

"I'm okay, darn it," Ben said. "I coulda took him."

"Yes you could," Laura said. She brushed the hair out of Ben's eyes and kissed him. She looked at Cordell. "Thank you, Mr. Cordell. It was a very brave thing you did."

They took Ben into the beanery in the mercantile and sat him down in a chair.

"Get food in him," Cordell said. "It'll do him some good."

Ben shook Cordell's hand. "I'm much obliged to ya fer backin' me up, mister. I guess I was in a tight spot."

"I always did want to shoot a politician and get away with it," Cordell said.

"Well, you sure did, partner," the cowboy said. "You sure did."

Sarah came in with Cordell's coat. She helped him put it on.

"I knew you was somethin' special the first time I saw yer pretty face, mister," she purred, "I surely did.

Cordell looked into her eyes. "Let's go for a walk."

"Sure. Where?"

"My horse is tied up on the hill," Cordell said. "I forgot all about him."

"Ya never want ta forget yer horse, mister. Or yer girl," Sarah said as they walked out into the yard and up the rise. "You ain't got no girlfriend, have ya?"

"What? After all we've been through. I thought you were the one." Then he said, "And I want my wallet back."

"I spent some of it," Sarah said.

"Then you owe me."

"I'm plumb broke, Mr. Cordell," Sarah said. "There ain't no way I kin pay you."

"Don't worry, I'll find a way."

When they got to the top of the rise, Cordell put his hands under Sarah's arms and picked her up, holding her high.

"Oh, my, sir! What are you gonna do ta me?" she said softly. They kissed.

Cordell set her on the saddle, and took the reins of his horse and led it into the woods.

14.

There were many bodies to bury and most of them were from Gadden's gang. Even with the entire posse digging, it took most of the day.

The Sheriff got a ledger from Corey Spencer and recorded the names of the deceased who had identification, and a description of those who didn't. He also took statements from Spencer and the defenders of the mercantile.

They buried Slade, Gadden, and the Senator in separate graves. The sheriff took Corey Spencer aside and spoke to him.

"Corey," Sheriff Cody said, "if you don't straighten up I'm gonna come up here and burn this place down. You know what I mean? Do I have to spell it out?"

"No, Sheriff," Spencer said.

He went and got the sack of loot from where he stashed it in the storeroom safe and handed it to the Sheriff.

"It's the stuff Slade gave me from thet last train he robbed."

The Sheriff took the bag and nodded. "That's a good start, Corey. A good start."

"I ain't doin' this anymore," Corey said, pointing at the sack. "It jest ain't worth it, what with all the runnin' around and all. No sir, Sheriff, I quit."

The Sheriff nodded. "I believe ya, friend."

The posse camped out on the porch and in the morning Spencer had the cook ready with a pay as you eat, self-serve breakfast. The hat at the end of the table quickly filled up.

After breakfast, the Sheriff cornered Cordell.

"What you said about Mungo, Bull, and Lackey, Cordell? Was thet the truth?"

"Yes. Every word, Sheriff."

"Well, you'll need ta go with me and the boys ta find those bodies and take them into Junction City, if you want the reward."

"All three thousand?" Cordell asked.

"Yep. All three thousand."

"Alright. Let me pack some food and water," Cordell said. "And talk to a certain girl."

"Go ahead. We'll leave in about an hour."

Cordell went into the mercantile for supplies. Laura Crowley and Sarah came from the restaurant to see him.

"You made me a widow, Mr. Cordell," Laura said. "I'm not a bit sorry about that."

"I didn't think you would be, ma'am, seeing as you're attached to the cowboy. So, what are your plans?"

"The ranch outside Hays City will be mine, now. I'll wire my parents to come and help me sort things out. I'll take Ben, Torrey, and Sarah with me."

"You know who they are, don't you?"

"Were, not are. Yes, but that's all in the past. They need a new start."

"That's very good of you, ma'am," Cordell said.

"You're welcome to come too, if you wish."

"Thank you."

Laura Crowley went back into the restaurant. Sarah looked at Cordell.

"You ain't runnin' out on me, are you?

"Running out? On you? Of course not."

"I see you packing yer saddle bag, so I figured you was hittin' the trail. Alone."

"No, no," Cordell said. "But I will be going with the Sheriff for a week. Maybe longer. To collect the three thousand reward."

"I won't be here when ya git back."

"I know. You'll be at Mrs. Crowley's ranch. Right?"

"Yep."

Cordell took some money from his billfold and handed it to Sarah.

"No."

"Yes. Buy a fancy dress."

"I don't need a fancy dress. I'm a cowgirl."

"But you'll need a dress."

"Why?"

"Because I'll come and take you dancing."

"You will?"

"Yes."

"Is thet a promise?"

"Yes. It's a promise."

"Alright. Then you buy the dress."

"What color?"

"Blue. Like the sky."

There were tears in Sarah's eyes. She reached up, pulled Cordell's face down to her face and kissed him. Then turned and ran into the restaurant.

Cordell took his saddlebag full of food and two canteens of water out to his horse and mounted up. The Sheriff gave the signal and they followed the trail heading east out of Sanctuary City. One of his deputies took up the rear with two packhorses.

Cordell looked back. Sarah, Laura and Ben were standing in the yard watching. He waved to them. They waved back. In a few moments the posse went down a slope and he couldn't see Sanctuary City anymore.

15.

When County Sheriff Frank Cody was notified that Senator Arnold Crowley's wife was kidnapped during a train robbery and there was a two thousand dollar reward for her return, he immediately formed a posse.

He sent his two deputies out to the Cattlemen's Association Building where cowboys looking for a job hung out and to the stockyards by the railroad. The word quickly spread and some of the saloon elements saw a chance to make some big money. In short order Sheriff Cody had his posse. He was pleased with the quick response. As for the seedy elements in the posse, Sheriff Cody didn't know how many or who they were.

When the posse left Sanctuary City, the Sheriff and Cordell took the lead.

"If yer ever looking for honest work, Cordell," the Sheriff said, "look me up."

"Thanks for the offer, Sheriff. I'm honored."

Cordell noticed how a small clique of riders hung back. There was something going on with them, he was sure. He thought about mentioning it to the Sheriff, but held off, waiting for the right moment.

"Sheriff, where'd you get your men?"

"The posse? From the town. I put out the word an' they came running fer the big reward."

"Do you know any by name?"

The Sheriff suddenly looked irritated. "I know a few. Why?"

"Nothing. Just talking."

"Well, don't talk so much." The Sheriff gave Cordell a cold look. "Keep movin' and stay in the lead."

The Sheriff fell back to ride alongside a man he knew.

One of the cowboys in the rear rode up beside Cordell.

"Hi! You're Cordell ain't ya?"

"Yes. That's me."

"What happened with thet reward fer the Senator's wife?"

"It didn't pan out."

"Yeah, because you drilled the Senator an' she ran off with thet cowboy."

"What's your point?" Cordell asked.

The cowboy chuckled. He wiped his nose with the back of his hand and sniffed.

"You'll find out, an' real soon, mister!"

Before Cordell could answer the man rode back to his buddies. A few moments later he heard them laughing. He glanced back and made a quick count. There were six of them.

That first night they made camp near a stream in a stand of pines. Cordell joined the Sheriff and the three cowboys he knew. They were friendly so he stayed with them for the rest of the night.

For the next two days it rained hard. It slowed them down. A few of the cowboys weren't too happy with how things had gone at Sanctuary City and how the Sheriff had been handling things. Some started to needle him. He shrugged it off.

Pretty soon everybody was on edge, including the Sheriff. The men started to grumble amongst themselves.

They rode all the way to Sanctuary city expecting to share in a two thousand dollar reward only to see it vanish before their very eyes when Cordell killed Senator Andrew Crowley. And now they were going back to Junction City with their pockets empty.

The next day a fight broke out between one of the suspicious acting cowboys and one of the Sheriff's friends. The suspicious cowboy lost. They buried him alongside the trail and went on. The other five didn't look too happy. They stayed off by themselves.

The following morning the Sheriff made a decision. This was no longer a posse but a bunch of angry men. Sheriff Cody gathered them all together.

"Men," the Sheriff said, "you all go on back to Junction City without me. I'm slowin' you down and I know some of you are anxious to see yer families and girlfriends agin. When I git back ta town I'll see you all get yer five dollars a day posse money, an' a little extra, too."

"Sounds good ta me," someone yelled and rode off for Junction City.

A second one said, "I had my fill of this crap! I'm a headin' home ta momma an' the kids! Come on, boys."

116

They all rode off leaving Cordell and the Sheriff alone with the two packhorses.

"Alright, Cordell," the Sheriff said. "How far to those bodies?"

Cordell chuckled and pointed upward.

16.

The Sheriff looked up. The first thing he noticed was the big, black birds circling over to the north. He nodded.

"About a day's ride?" he asked.

"About that," Cordell said.

They rode on. By dark they were almost there but decided to camp. They didn't find a stream but the packhorses had water bags with enough water for a pot of coffee. They ate jerky and hard tack and rolled out their blankets.

"They can't be much left to them three by now," the sheriff said.

"I hope not, Cordell said, "I don't want to be hauling any rotten meat around."

"Yeah. Good thinkin'," the Marshall said, chuckling. "Well, good night, Cordell."

They rose early, broke camp and started off to find a stream. After about two miles they came to one and stopped to make coffee. They ate breakfast and moved on.

Finally they were near where the buzzards were feeding. In another mile they could smell the stench of rotting flesh. They came up to where the bodies lay. There wasn't much left.

"We'll take what's left of the clothing," the Sheriff said. "Just to show as evidence for yer claim on the bounty"

"Good idea," Cordell said.

They went over to the bodies and picked up as many pieces of prison clothing as they could. The rain had washed most of it, so it didn't smell too bad. They put it all in a saddlebag on one of the packhorses. It took about an hour to get what they needed.

As they were about to mount up, Cordell froze. There, twenty yards away were mounted men. As they came closer Cordell counted five. He recognized them from the posse, the suspicious ones. The one who had talked to him was the leader. They spread out as they came on, stopping a few yards away.

Cordell quickly sized them up. The one on Cordell's far left was the youngest. Even for all of his young years he looked dull-eyed, emotionless and cold. To the young man's left was a middle-aged man just as hard faced and to the left of him was an older man. He looked like he'd seen a lot of action. He had a sneer on his lips. To his left was the leader and another man who was a bit on the heavy side. He chewed tobacco and spit juice. He had a nervous tic in his left eye.

"Well, well," the leader said. "What have we got here, men?" The others sort of snickered. "It looks like the good Sheriff here is tryin' ta pull a fast one. Are you tryin' ta pull a fast one, Sheriff?"

"Nobody is trying to pull anything," the Sheriff said.

"Well it looks ta me like you two are out ta collect the three grand on those escaped convicts we heard about."

"The reward belongs to Cordell, here," the Sheriff said. "It was him who killed the three of them. He did the job so he gets the money. Thet's only right, isn't it?"

The leader chuckled. "It is if he delivers the evidence, Sheriff. But I don't think he's gonna make it back to Junction City. An' neither are you, for thet matter."

A buzzard floated down intending to have a meal but when it saw the humans, he flapped his wings and went upward again.

The young man chuckled.

"They'll have plenty ta eat in a while, won't they boss?"

"They sure will, kid," the leader said.

Cordell looked across at the young kid.

"Kid, if I were you I'd go back to Junction City and collect the posse reward. Take your girl to a dance. You're gonna die here."

The kid sneered and spit off to one side.

"The hell you say!" He glared at Cordell. "Who do you think you are, my pappy?"

"He's Jack Cordell," the Sheriff said. "He outdrew Red Hardy some years ago. But yer a greenhorn, so maybe it don't mean nothin' to you."

The leader sneered. "Oh, yeah. I heard about thet. You got lucky, they say."

"Maybe," Cordell said, "but I'm still alive to talk about it and he isn't. And if you draw, it'll be your last one."

The leader looked at his companions.

"Did you hear thet, boys? Him with an old broke down Sheriff facin' the five of us, and he's a braggin' about how good he is? That takes balls! Haw!"

Without warning the leader drew and then everybody drew.

The woods shook with the roar of gunfire. Terrified birds darted skyward in a burst of speed. The buzzards moved higher to watch from above.

The Sheriff dipped low as he drew and fired upward, fanning the hammer of his gun. He knew his targets were to the right and Cordell's were to the left. He'd been in this situation a dozen times. He shot the tobacco chewer in the chest, knocking him out of the saddle just as the leader put a slug in his left leg. The Sheriff went down on his one good knee with a grunt and shot back, putting a bullet between the leader's eyes.

Cordell jumped to the right and fired while in motion. He shot the middle-aged outlaw in the shoulder, and the older one in the chest. As he landed on his bent knees, the kid put a bullet in his left arm near the elbow. Cordell fired back and hit the kid in the chest then finished off the middle-aged man with a shot to the heart as the kid slipped backward over his horse and hit the ground.

One of the outlaw's horses whinnied and ran off frightened. The Sheriff and Cordell knelt on the ground reloading. They pointed their guns at where the attackers had been, then realized it was all over. The sound of gunfire faded away. In its place was the wind moaning high in the pine trees. Crows cawed somewhere in the distance.

"Sweet Jesus!" Sheriff Cody said. "I can't take much more of this. He stood up and suddenly realized he had been shot in the left thigh. He looked at it.

"Bad?" Cordell asked.

"I've had worse. You?"

"Not so bad."

The Sheriff limped over to one of the packhorses and got out the medicine box and wrapped his leg. When he was finished he tossed the roll of bandage to Cordell. He laughed.

"What's so funny?" Cordell asked, as he wrapped his arm.

"Me. You. The both of us," the Sheriff chuckled. "We sure are two lucky sons a bitches. We should be layin' here dead as a doornail. But we ain't."

"You got any whiskey on those packhorses. Sheriff? If you do, this might be a good time for a drink."

"Fer a drunk is more like it," the Sheriff said.

He went to one of the packhorses and got a bottle of whiskey. They found a windfall and sat down to drink.

"I sure wish you'd sign on with me, Cordell," Sheriff Cody said. "I would be honored if ya did."

"I'd be honored too, Sheriff," Cordell said. "But I've got a date with a little buck-tooth beauty over by Hays City."

"I see."

"But thanks for asking. I do feel honored."

After a while, when the whiskey burned out the chill, they got up.

"What's next, Sheriff?" Cordell asked.

"We'll tie their horses to the pack animals and take them with us. I'm gonna sell 'em for what I kin get, saddles an' all."

"The bodies?"

"Let the buzzards an' crows fight over 'em."

In a short while they left. The Sheriff began to sing 'Amazing Grace'. He was half-drunk and so was Cordell.

17.

Senator Crowley's ranch, the Circle C, lay abut forty miles northwest of Hays City on the Kansas plains. With about seven thousand square acres or about ten square miles, it was a small ranch. It had about four thousand head of cattle, good open grazing and plenty of water. Hills of scrub oak, fields of prairie grass, and stands of pine and aspen gave it a picturesque look.

Now it belonged to Laura Crowley.

Of all the short years she was married to the Senator, she hadn't spent very much time at the ranch but she did know that although he was feared, he wasn't very much liked or respected. Many of those at the ranch watched him grow up and saw his sadistic nature and his disregard for life, animal and human.

To them, Laura was a breath of fresh air. They loved and welcomed this refined, educated, sensitive girl.

When news of the Senator's death in a gun duel reached the ranch days before Laura did, there was a collective sigh of relief as if a heavy yoke had been lifted. They would no longer have to put up with the Senator's oppressive ways. And that was cause for elation and celebration.

A story also reached the ranch about outlaws kidnapping Laura from the train and taking her to a place called Sanctuary City and demanding a ransom of ten thousand dollars for her release. The story also told how a young cowboy and his friends came to her rescue and killed the outlaws.

This story soon reached the newspapers in Hays City and other cities along the Union Pacific Railroad. Pulp magazines picked it up, embellished it and ran with it. It sold well even thought it was romanticized far beyond the truth. Laura would later buy copies of those penny dreadful pulps and read them to Ben, Torrey and Sarah for their enjoyment.

As far as the Senator was concerned, the newspapers reported that the Senator had been insulted by a man named Jack Cordell and challenged him to a duel and been killed. It mentioned Laura as his surviving widow. It praised the Senator as an important rising star in the political world. He would be sorely missed. People could visit his gravesite at a place called Sanctuary City.

When Laura finally arrived at the Circle C Ranch with Ben, Torrey and Sarah, eyebrows were raised. Once they realized these three young people were the very ones who rescued their mistress, they welcomed them with open hearts and arms.

Torrey hired on as a cowboy, getting back to his roots. Ben and Laura planned to get married the following year but in the meantime, he would get to cowboy as much as he wanted to. This simple, good-hearted man was soon loved by all. Sarah became Laura's companion.

Two weeks after arriving at the Circle C, Sarah took Laura aside.

"I'll be leaving, soon, Miss Laura," Sarah said. "I can't stay here."

"But why not?"

"He said he'd come and take me to a dance. Well, it looks like he ain't gonna."

"Give it more time. It's only been two weeks now."

"He woulda come by now, if he'd a wanted to."

"Please stay," Laura said. "I need you here with me. You're my very dear friend. I love you like a sister."

"Please don't say thet, ma'am. It makes it harder ta go."

They held each other and cried.

Early the next day Sarah mounted up and rode out without saying goodbye. She rode up a hill a mile from the ranch and stopped to look down. She started to cry. Everyone she loved was back there. She had no one and nothing now.

She sighed and turned away.

As she did, she saw a dot moving just over the far horizon. It was coming fast in her direction against a blue sky and white clouds. It suddenly stopped and moments later, it was waving a blue flag in the wind. As it came closer, the flag turned into a dress and the figure became Jack Cordell.

Sarah urged her horse into a full gallop and headed straight at Cordell. They met in a small bowl of grass, reached out to grab each other, and fell off their horses, locked in each other's arms.

"Is thet the dress you promised me, Mr. Cordell, sir?" Sarah asked.

"It is," Cordell said. "Why are you crying?"

"I thought you'd forgot all about your Buck-tooth Sarah. How come you took so long?"

"I had to collect a three thousand reward for some work I did. It took a little while."

"You ain't gonna leave me agin, are ya?"

"Maybe someday," Cordell said. "But not for a while."

"You gonna take me to a dance?"

"I'll take you to a hundred dances," Cordell said. He kissed Sarah's forehead, eyes, nose and mouth.

Sarah grabbed her blue dress and they mounted up and rode back towards the Circle C.

The End.

About the Author

R. Annan is a seasoned and traveled author with many interests. As a career service man, he served in Korea and Vietnam. He also completed a one-year course at the Defense Language Institute at Monterey, California, and graduated from the University of South Florida with a B.A. in Art and Art History. After taking a two-year course in screenwriting at the Hollywood Scriptwriting Institute, he established The Old Time Radio Club Time Machine as both a scriptwriter and an actor.

A Note from the Author

Thank you for reading my book. If you enjoyed it, would you please consider rating and reviewing it? I'd enjoy your feedback.

Look for other books to appear soon by following me on my Author Page. Thank you!